BEATRIX POTTER

written and illustrated by

ALEXANDRA WALLNER

Holiday House/New York

Library of Congress Cataloging-in-Publication Data
Wallner, Alexandra.
Beatrix Potter / written and illustrated by Alexandra Wallner.
p.   cm.
ISBN 0-8234-1181-8
1. Potter, Beatrix, 1866–1943—Biography—Juvenile literature.
2. Women authors, English—20th century—Biography—Juvenile
literature.   3. Women artists—Great Britain—Biography—Juvenile
literature. [1. Potter, Beatrix, 1866–1943.   2. Authors, English.
3. Artists.   4. Women—Biography.]   I. Title.
PR6031.072Z96   1995   94-41238   CIP   AC
823′.912—dc20
[B]
ISBN 0-8234-1407-8 (pbk.)

ISBN-13: 978-0-8234-1181-8 (hardcover)   ISBN-10: 0-8234-1181-8 (hardcover)
ISBN-13: 978-0-8234-1407-9 (pbk.)   ISBN-10: 0-8234-1407-8 (pbk.)

"I have just made stories to please myself, because I never grew up."
—Beatrix Potter

For John~
A.C.W.

Helen Beatrix Potter was born in London, England on July 28, 1866. She was the first child of her parents, Rupert and Helen Potter. Her brother Bertram was born five years later.

Like many children in wealthy English families, Beatrix and Bertram didn't see much of their parents. They were left in the care of governesses.

Instead of going to school, they had their lessons at home. They hardly saw other children. Occasionally, their parents allowed them to play with cousins.

Beatrix and Bertram were lonely. They spent a lot of time drawing and painting flowers and animals. Their many pets became their only friends. Without the adults knowing, they hid rabbits, frogs, lizards, newts, snakes, salamanders, bats, mice, and a turtle. Even after the pets died, they saved the skeletons and drew the bones.

Beatrix was especially fond of two pet mice named Hunca Munca and Appley Dapply, and a rabbit named Peter.

Mr. and Mrs. Potter encouraged Beatrix and Bertram to study art. Beatrix's father enjoyed photography and collected paintings. When Beatrix was old enough, he took her to museums. He introduced her to John Everett Millais, a famous painter, who showed her his studio. Thanks to her father, Beatrix saw how an artist lived and worked.

In the summers Beatrix went to Scotland with her family. The Potters rented different houses near the woods. Beatrix kept a diary written in her own code. The sights and sounds of the woods were like magic to her and ". . . everything was romantic in my imagination." She also liked to paint wildflowers and small woodland animals. Her years of practice made her an excellent painter.

When Beatrix was seventeen, her parents sent Bertram to boarding school. Now she was lonelier than ever.

Her mother hired Annie Carter to be her companion. Annie was only three years older than Beatrix. It was the first time Beatrix had a girlfriend. She loved Annie and enjoyed her company. But two years later Annie got married and moved away.

Beatrix was alone again. She wrote, "I cannot rest, I must draw . . . when I have a bad time come over me it is a stronger desire than ever." Bad times came over her often. Throughout her life she had periods of bronchitis and rheumatic fever which left her heart weak.

Her mother and father were strict. As Beatrix grew older, she wished she could make her own decisions.

Beatrix got a pet rabbit and named him "Bounce." She painted him from all angles wearing human clothes, as if he were a person. A greeting card company bought some of these paintings. They were published along with some verses in a booklet called *A Happy Pair*. But the money she earned from that was not enough to support herself. She still had to live with her parents.

One night, when Beatrix was particularly lonely and there was no one to talk to, she wrote a letter to a little boy named Noel. He was the son of her former companion, Annie Carter.

"My Dear Noel,
I don't know what to write to you, so I shall tell you a story about four little rabbits whose names are Flopsy, Mopsy, Cottontail and Peter."

She wrote the first version of *The Tale of Peter Rabbit*, although she didn't know it at the time. She didn't think about writing other stories because she was more interested in making drawings and keeping notes on science.

When Beatrix was in her twenties, she painted the mushrooms she had collected in Scotland during her summer vacations. She had learned a great deal about them. She noted in her diary that rotted mushrooms might be used in cancer research.

Beatrix wanted to publish a report and sell the 300 paintings of mushrooms she had completed. Sadly, her research was not taken seriously. Because she lived at a time when men considered themselves the experts in the study of science, her work was not accepted. Beatrix was hurt because she felt she knew more about mushrooms than almost anyone in England.

Again Beatrix turned to animals for comfort. She borrowed back the letter she had written to Noel, rewriting the story about the four little rabbits.

Although she sent it to several publishers, none wanted it. Beatrix did not give up. In 1901, she decided to have 250 copies of the story printed herself.

Beatrix gave them to friends. The rest she left with local bookstores. She was encouraged when they quickly sold out. An editor at Frederick Warne Publishers saw one of the books. He wanted her to make the drawings larger and to rewrite the story.

Beatrix was excited. She agreed to rewrite the text but would not enlarge the pictures. The book needed to be small, she told him, so that children's hands could hold it easily.

Beatrix got her way and *The Tale of Peter Rabbit* was published in 1902 when Beatrix was thirty-six years old. The book was very popular and made a lot of money for her.

In 1905, Beatrix bought Hilltop Farm in the rural Lake District of England. But Beatrix remained living at home, because that was expected of an unmarried daughter. When she could get away from her parents, she stayed at Hilltop and wrote tales of mice, rabbits, squirrels, foxes, cats, dogs, and farm animals. She remembered how lonely she had been as a child. Animals had always made her feel better. She wanted to write about her animal friends for other lonely children. She wrote of a pet hedgehog named Mrs. Tiggy-Winkle and a pet duck called Jemima Puddle-Duck.

When Beatrix wasn't writing, she tended her garden and took care of her animals. She kept cows, sheep, pigs, and chickens. Finally, Beatrix was doing what she wanted and was happy.

Beatrix sent her stories to Norman Warne, who was now her editor.
They wrote many letters to each other. After a while they fell in love.

In 1905, Norman proposed to Beatrix. Although her parents did not want her to marry, she accepted. But she never married Norman. Suddenly he became sick and died.

Beatrix was very sad. She spent a lot of time writing more stories. All of her books were popular.

In 1909, Beatrix bought another farm called Castle Cottage. During the purchase, she met a lawyer named William Heelis. They both enjoyed animals and farming. They fell in love and were engaged in 1912.

Again Mr. and Mrs. Potter disapproved. Even so, in 1913, Beatrix married William, and they moved to Castle Cottage.

Beatrix was happy with William. She wasn't lonely anymore. After her marriage, she hardly wrote and painted at all. Her eyesight was getting weak, and she preferred spending her time with her animals and farming.

Beatrix bought many surrounding farms and turned the houses into museums. She also wanted to keep the woods and fields the way they were, so she had footpaths created for the tourists who visited the lakes. This way they would not step on the wildflowers and disturb the small animals in their homes.

As Beatrix grew older, she spent most of her time raising Herdwick sheep. They won many prizes at the local county fairs. The Herdwick Sheepbreeders' Association elected her as their first and only woman president.

Beatrix died on December 22, 1943 at the age of seventy-seven. She had written twenty-three "tales" and other books which were read by children around the world. Even though Beatrix was famous, she remained private and modest.

"If I have done anything—even a little to help small children on the road to enjoy and appreciate honest, simple pleasures, I have done a bit of good," she said.

Author's Note

Although Beatrix never saw her fungi paintings printed, in 1966 fifty-nine of them were published in a book, *Wayside and Woodland Fungi.*

Experiments with fungi were done in Russia for cancer research many years after Beatrix had suggested rotted mushrooms might lead to a cure.

When Beatrix died she left over 4,000 acres of farms, pastures, and woods to the National Trust that protects land in England. Visitors can see how rural people of the last two centuries lived because of the museums she created.

Beatrix's original paintings can still be seen at Hilltop Farm in Sawrey, England.

Although Beatrix Potter wrote a few other books, her twenty-three "tales" are the most famous. They are:

The Tale of Peter Rabbit
The Tale of Squirrel Nutkin
The Tailor of Gloucester
The Tale of Benjamin Bunny
The Tale of Two Bad Mice
The Tale of Mrs. Tiggy-Winkle
The Tale of The Pie and The
   Patty-Pan
The Tale of Mr. Jeremy Fisher
The Story of A Fierce Bad Rabbit
The Story of Miss Moppet
The Tale of Tom Kitten
The Tale of Jemima Puddle-Duck

The Tale of Samuel Whiskers or
   The Roly-Poly Pudding
The Tale of The Flopsy Bunnies
The Tale of Ginger and Pickles
The Tale of Mrs. Tittlemouse
The Tale of Timmy Tiptoes
The Tale of Mr. Tod
The Tale of Pigling Bland
Appley Dapply's Nursery Rhymes
The Tale of Johnny Town-Mouse
Cecily Parsley's Nursery Rhymes
The Tale of Little Pig Robinson